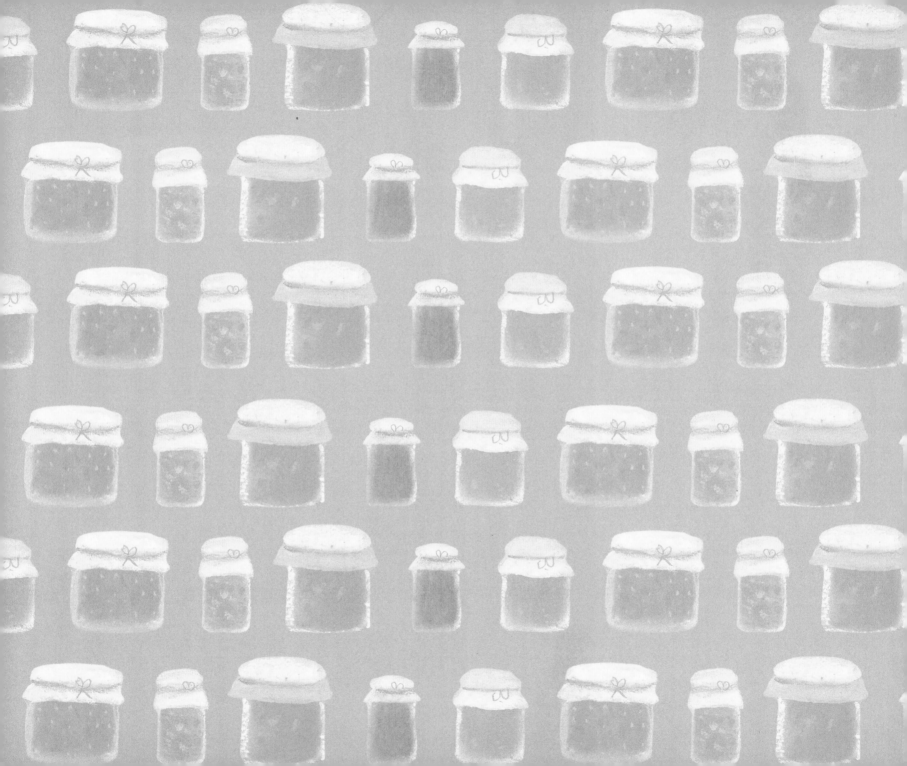

Everyone
Needs a Friend

PRICE STERN SLOAN
Published by the Penguin Group
Penguin Group (USA) Inc., 375 Hudson Street, New York, New York 10014, USA
Penguin Group (Canada), 90 Eglinton Avenue East, Suite 700,
Toronto, Ontario M4P 2Y3, Canada
(a division of Pearson Penguin Canada Inc.)
Penguin Books Ltd., 80 Strand, London WC2R 0RL, England
Penguin Group Ireland, 25 St. Stephen's Green, Dublin 2, Ireland
(a division of Penguin Books Ltd.)
Penguin Group (Australia), 250 Camberwell Road, Camberwell, Victoria 3124, Australia
(a division of Pearson Australia Group Pty. Ltd.)
Penguin Books India Pvt. Ltd., 11 Community Centre,
Panchsheel Park, New Delhi—110 017, India
Penguin Group (NZ), 67 Apollo Drive, Rosedale, North Shore 0632, New Zealand
(a division of Pearson New Zealand Ltd.)
Penguin Books (South Africa) (Pty.) Ltd., 24 Sturdee Avenue,
Rosebank, Johannesburg 2196, South Africa

Penguin Books Ltd., Registered Offices:
80 Strand, London WC2R 0RL, England

Library of Congress Cataloging-in-Publication Data is available.

ISBN 978-0-8431-9918-5   10 9 8 7 6 5 4 3 2 1

Everyone
Needs a Friend

by Dubravka Kolanovic

PSS!

PRICE STERN SLOAN

An Imprint of Penguin Group (USA) Inc.

Jack the wolf lived all alone in a
small house far up in the hills.

In the summertime, Jack went for
long walks in the forest and picked
huge baskets of juicy berries.

In the fall, Jack made jam. He filled his
pantry with colorful jars of raspberry,
strawberry, and blueberry jam.

In the winter, when it was cold and snowy outside, Jack stayed indoors. He kept himself busy knitting warm, colorful scarves.

Jack loved his small
house in the hills.
But sometimes living
all alone got lonely!

Then one night a visitor came to
Jack's house. It was Walter the
mouse. He was lost and looking
for a place to spend the night.

Jack happily invited Walter in.
The next morning, Jack made a
big breakfast for his new friend.
Cocoa and toast with his
best jar of jam!

When they finished eating,
Jack and Walter went
outside to build snowmen.

Jack had forgotten how much fun
it could be to play with a friend!

At bedtime, it was still snowing hard.
Jack invited Walter to stay for another night.
But that night Jack could not sleep. For a very
small mouse, Walter had a very LOUD snore!

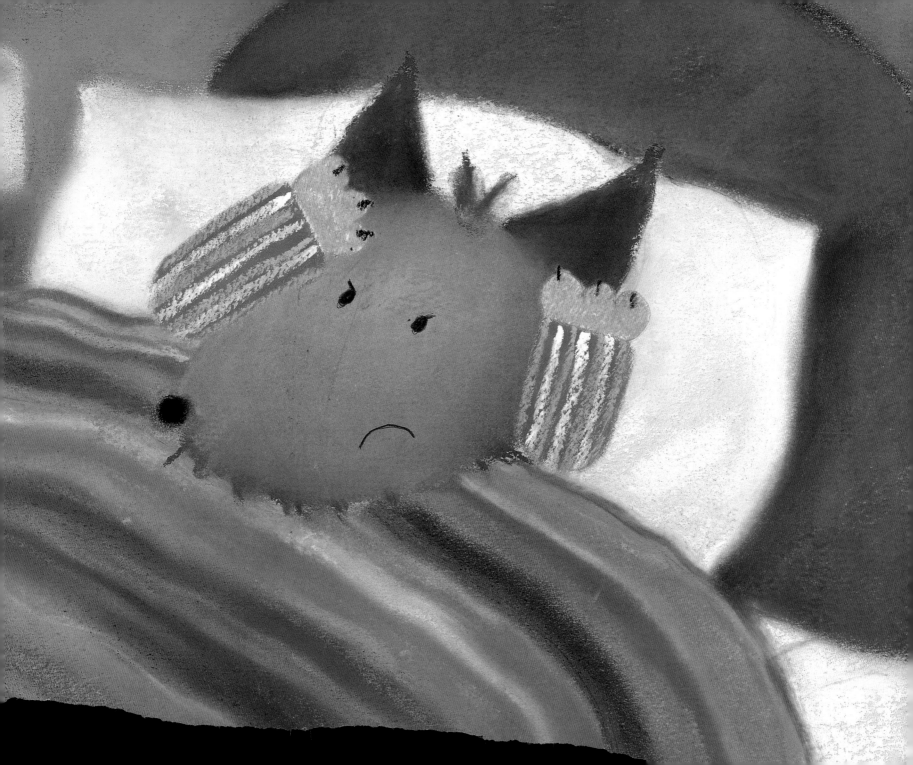

The next morning, Jack was tired and grumpy.
When he got to the kitchen, he saw that
Walter had started breakfast without him.
There was jam everywhere!

After breakfast, Walter needed a nap. He crept
inside Jack's balls of yarn and fell asleep.

When Jack saw what a mess Walter had
made, he became very angry!

Walter tried to apologize, but Jack
was too angry to listen. He yelled at
Walter and asked him to leave.

But as Jack watched Walter walk away, he began to feel sorry. He remembered how lonely life had been without Walter and the fun they had had together.

Jack grabbed his favorite scarf
and ran after Walter. "Come back!" he cried.

When Jack caught up with Walter,
he wrapped him up in the soft, warm scarf.
Then he apologized and asked
Walter to come home.

Walter agreed and came to live
with Jack. All winter, and into
the spring, he learned how
to knit and make jam.

And Jack learned that no matter how big a mess Walter made, it was worth it to have his friend around!

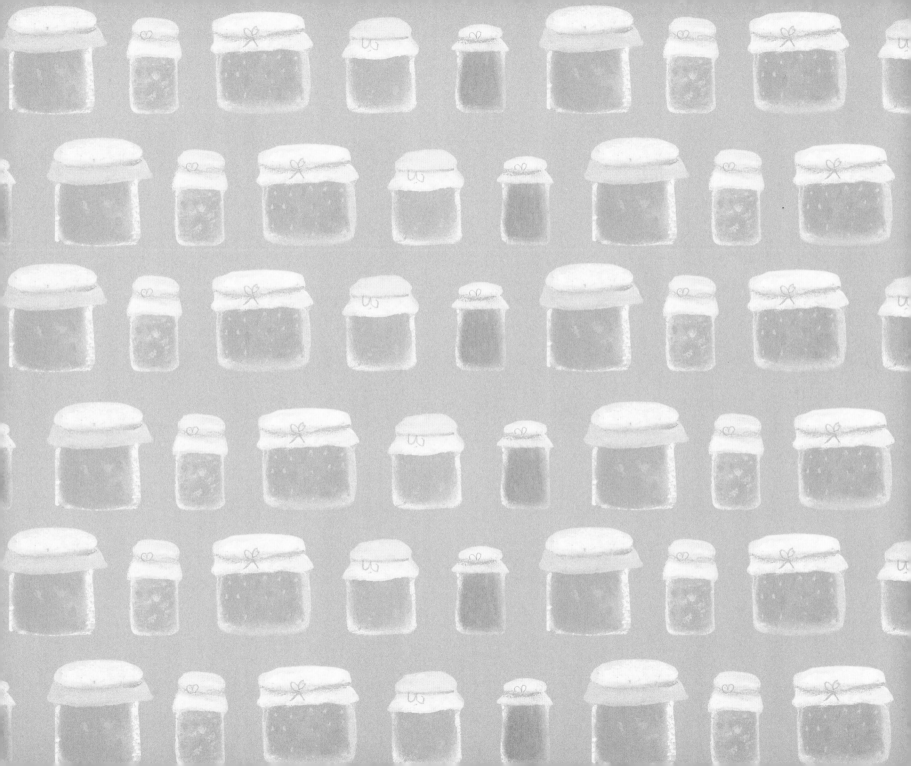

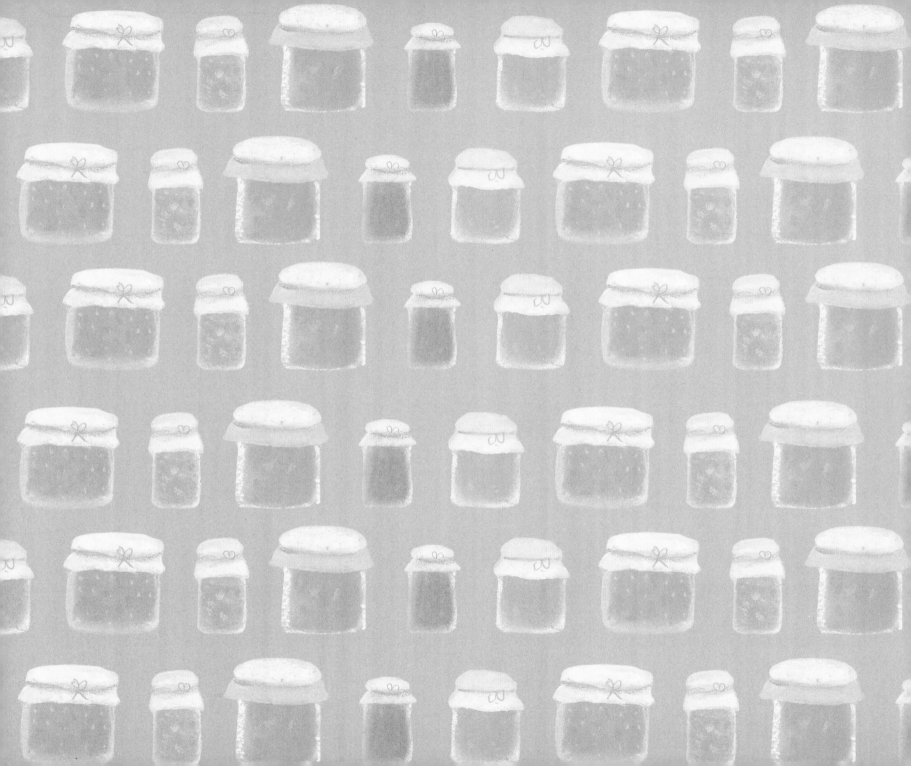